The Sleepover Club

Have you been invited to all these sleepovers?

The Sleepover Club
at the Carnival

by Sue Mongredien

An imprint of HarperCollinsPublishers

The Sleepover Club ® is a
registered trademark of HarperCollins*Publishers* Ltd

First published in Great Britain by Collins in 2001
Collins is an imprint of HarperCollins*Publishers* Ltd
77-85 Fulham Palace Road, Hammersmith,
London, W6 8JB

The HarperCollins website address is
www.**fire**and**water**.com

1 3 5 7 9 8 6 4 2

Text copyright © Sue Mongredien 2001

Original series characters, plotlines
and settings © Rose Impey 1997

ISBN 0 00710540 1

The author asserts the moral right to
be identified as the author of the work.

Printed and bound in Great Britain by
Omnia Books Limited, Glasgow

Sleepover Kit List

1. Sleeping bag
2. Pillow
3. Pyjamas or a nightdress
4. Slippers
5. Toothbrush, toothpaste, soap etc
6. Towel
7. Teddy
8. A creepy story
9. Food for a midnight feast:
   chocolate, crisps, sweets, biscuits.
   In fact anything you like to eat.
10. Torch
11. Hairbrush
12. Hair things like a bobble or hairband,
    if you need them
13. Clean knickers and socks
14. Change of clothes for the next day
15. Sleepover diary and membership card

CHAPTER ONE

Howdy, fans, Kenny here. You know, the quiet, shy, retiring, polite one! What do you mean, you don't believe me? Oh, OK, then – I'm the loud, rude one who's always getting us into trouble. Satisfied?

Hey, what are you doing upside-down like that anyway? What? You're NOT upside-down? Oh – silly me! You just LOOK upside-down, that's all. In fact, everything looks upside-down – because *I'm* upside-down! Derrr! I've been practising for the world record in standing on your head, you see. The only thing is, after a while, you forget you're the wrong way round and it seems perfectly normal to be staring at people's feet. My dad keeps saying that being upside-down all the time means my brain is getting squashed, and it's only a matter of time before it turns to mush. I don't THINK I believe him, but then he IS a doctor, so maybe he knows something I don't?

Hang on a second while I turn the right way again. There, that's better! Let's go and sit out in the garden, shall we? I hate staying indoors when the weather's nice. Why stay inside four boring walls when you can practise your cartwheels up and down the lawn?

Anyway, I'm glad I saw you, because the others voted for me to tell you all about the Cuddington Carnival and what we did for it. "Kenny," they said, "as the best, funniest, cleverest and most entertaining storyteller of all of us, you MUST tell all the Sleepover Club fans what happened at the carnival. We're begging you!"

OK, OK, so the others didn't *quite* say all of that. But as Frankie pointed out, a lot of what

I'm about to tell you is MY story. And as animal-mad Lyndz would say – you might as well hear it straight from the horse's mouth! (Not that I'm a horse, but... Oh, you know what I mean.)

Have you ever been to a carnival? Believe it or not, I HADN'T until last week. Now I've been to one, I want to go to lots more – they are so megatastically awesome! And the only thing that's keeping me from being completely gutted that this year's carnival is all over, is the fact that it's half term now. We're off school for a week, yippee! But if the carnival had just finished and we still had to go back to school – that would just be too traumatic for words!

Anyway, I'd better get on with the story. The rest of the Sleepover Club is coming over for lunch in a bit, and you know what a load of blabbermouths they are – they'll just want to interrupt me all the time. And we don't want that, do we?

Well, the first I heard about the Cuddington Carnival was from my mum. She's a pretty good source for juicy gossip, and always knows what's going on around Cuddington. She helps out as a receptionist at my dad's surgery and also does some hairdressing from home, so one way or another, people are always telling her their news – which she then tells to my grandma on the phone. That's when I start earwigging.

Over the years, I've built up quite a good gossip radar in my ears. There are certain words that my radar always picks up on, however boring the rest of the talk is. For example, here's a typical conversation between Mum and Grandma on the phone. Mum tends to do most of the talking so this is what I hear:

"Recipe for lemon cake... drone, drone... Alison Parker's new baby... drone, drone... Mrs Ellis's sciatica... drone, drone... Emma's boyfriend..."

PING! That's where my ears prick up. Emma's my oldest sister and she never tells me anything about her love life, even though I'm always trying to find out the gory details. Excellent blackmailing material, you see – not to mention all the fun I can have winding her up! But although Emma won't tell ME anything, she often confides in Mum, and that's where the gossip radar comes in handy. It means that once Mum starts yakking on to Grandma about it, yours truly gets to find out what's going on, too!

So a couple of weeks ago, I was sitting in my favourite eavesdropping position – at the kitchen table, pretending to flick through one of Emma's magazines, with one ear firmly tuned to Mum. This time, I heard:

"Cathy Clayton's new hairdo... drone, drone... Jim's working too hard... drone, drone... Molly's piano exam... drone, drone... plans for the carnival..."

PING! Carnival? What carnival? What was she talking about? I immediately tuned in fully to hear more.

"Yes, Sheila Adams told me about it," Mum was saying. "At the end of the month... Oh, you know, floats and dressing up and bouncy castles, I should think... Mmm, well, she's asked me to help out with some baking, as there are going to be stalls in the main street. I was wondering if I could get your chocolate cheesecake recipe off you... Yes..."

My radar switched itself off at the recipe word. Dull City! Then I had to wait impatiently while Mum finished chatting before I could find out any more about the carnival.

Click! The second that I heard her put the phone down, I swung round in my chair. "Mum, what were you saying about a carnival?" I said at once. "I couldn't help overhearing..."

She grinned at me. "I thought I could feel the breeze of a pair of ears flapping behind me," she said. She was pretending to be cross, but I knew she didn't mind. Let's face it, we both know where I get my nosiness from. "I was just telling Grandma that Cuddington is going to have a carnival at the end of the month. Something to do with Cuddington being one hundred years old. I'm going to be doing some baking for it, and—"

"But what IS a carnival exactly?" I burst out, not wanting to hear another word about Mum's baking plans. "I mean, what's going to be happening? Is it just a load of soppy dancing and stuff?"

14

She thought for a moment. "I think it's all a bit up in the air still," she said. "Yes, there'll be dancing and music and bands playing, I should think. Then there's probably going to be a parade with different floats, and people all dressed up. There's going to be a funfair on the green with lots of rides and a bouncy castle. And stalls and sideshows up and down the high street. That sort of thing."

I bounced off my chair and jumped up and down with excitement. "Excellent!" I said. "Wait till I tell the others!"

I was just about to get on the phone and ring round the rest of the Sleepover Club to tell them the news but Mum looked at her watch. "Not so fast," she said. "I promised Emma she could use the phone after I'd finished. And by the time SHE's done with it, it'll be your bedtime."

"Oh, Mu-um!" I moaned. Emma's sixteen and spends HOURS on the phone. It must be a weird teenage thing because Rosie's big sister Tiffany is exactly the same. Never mind my bedtime, it would practically be *breakfast* time by the time Emma had finished gassing away to her mates.

"I'm sure it can wait until school tomorrow," Mum said briskly. "And anyway, it's high time you had a bath, young lady. Look at the colour of your neck! What have you been doing – rolling around in mud or something?"

"Of course not!" I said grumpily, going up to the bathroom. Well, I wasn't about to tell her I'd been timing myself doing circuits of forward and backward rolls around the garden, was I? Especially as I'd managed to kick quite a lot of her flowers in the process.

So even though I was bursting to tell everyone about the carnival, I wasn't able to say anything until the next day at school. And even THEN, it didn't go according to plan.

I went up to school extra fast the next morning. Yeah, I know – that's not like me at all! Even though I'm pretty speedy on my feet most of the time, the journey to school somehow takes me a lot longer than if I'm going to the swimming baths or to a footy match or something. Strange, isn't it? It's as if my feet just can't bear to take me to such a boring place. Well, that's my theory anyway.

The others were already in the playground when I got there. "Hi!" I said excitedly, rushing over to them. "Guess what? I've got some wicked news to tell you!"

"What?" Frankie, Lyndz and Rosie said at once, but Fliss just frowned. "I was actually in the middle of telling everyone what the twins did last night," she said huffily. "So let me finish first!"

Frankie rolled her eyes at me, and Rosie bit her lip, trying not to giggle at the cross look on my face. Lyndz, who's definitely the most patient one of us five, was the only one listening to Fliss's boring story about what her baby sister and brother had been up to now.

"And you'll never guess where I found Hannah's rattle in the end," Fliss said at long last, building up to a dramatic climax. "In the fridge!"

"Really? In the fridge?" Lyndz asked. "How had it got in there?"

"Well," Fliss began – but Frankie was just a

smidgen too quick for her.

"C'mon, Kenz – what's your news? You look like you're about to burst with it!" she said.

"Get a load of this," I said importantly, "Mum told me last night that—"
PEEEEPPPP!

Curses! Now it was Mrs Poole our headteacher's turn to interrupt me, blowing the whistle to get us to line up and go into school.

"What is it?" hissed Frankie as we lined up in front of Mrs Weaver.

"Tell you later," I muttered out of the corner of my mouth. The Cuddington carnival wasn't something I wanted to whisper to the others just before we went into class. I needed time to tell them about it *properly*.

But then, wouldn't you know it? It just wasn't going to be my day for breaking the news. As soon as we'd had the register, Mrs Weaver smiled a big smile at us and said she had something exciting to tell us about. Then she pulled down the blackboard to show one word: CARNIVAL.

Aaaaarggghhh! So all in all, I'd been

scuppered by:

Emma – using the phone

Mum – who'd made me go to bed

Fliss – who wouldn't let me interrupt her boring story

Mrs Poole – blowing the whistle just at the crucial moment

And Mrs Weaver – telling everyone about the carnival before I could. Gutted!

CHAPTER TWO

I wasn't gutted for *too* long, of course. First, because I never stay in a mood for longer than about five minutes, and second, because Mrs Weaver had a lot more information about the carnival than my mum had.

For starters, she told us all about how *we* were going to get involved. "As well as bands, fairground rides and stalls, there will be a procession of floats along the high street," she said. "Each float has a particular theme. There'll be lots of people wearing costumes, and all the floats will be decorated differently. Best of all, Cuddington Primary School is going to have its own float – and it's going to be designed and decorated by YOU!"

Everyone looked excited at that. This sounded like fun!

"I haven't finished yet," she said, smiling. "The top classes – that's ours and Mr Phillips' class – are responsible for actually putting together the float. The younger classes are going to put together a display of pictures for the library. So I want you all to come up with a good theme for us to have for the float. Now..."

"Football!" Simon Graham said at once.

I grinned at him and gave him the thumbs-up. I'd be on for that one!

"Horse riding!" Lyndz blurted out eagerly.

"Harry Potter!" someone else shouted.

Mrs Weaver banged on the desk with her ruler. "Whoa, whoa, whoa!" she said. "There'll be plenty of time for your ideas later. Don't you think it would be a good idea to find out more about the carnival before you all start shouting things out?"

The classroom went quiet.

"Now," Mrs Weaver continued, "do you remember when it was the millennium and the whole world looked back over the last thousand years? Well, this year marks one HUNDRED years of Cuddington – as far as we can tell. Lots of the old buildings in the village were built in 1901 – for example, the main bank on the high street, the library, the old grammar school and most importantly, the big stone cross in the marketplace. 1901 also saw the beginning of the weekly farmers' market where local people could buy and sell pigs, sheep and cows, as well as fruit and vegetables. The market's a bit different these days, but it's still going strong, after all this time."

I looked at Lyndz, who had this dead wistful expression on her face. I just *knew* she was wishing that you could still buy piglets and lambs at Cuddington market. Lyndz is totally soppy about baby animals. Unfortunately, the market only sells things like tea towels and big granny pants these days.

"So that's the main reason for the carnival – it's to celebrate one hundred years of

Cuddington's history," Mrs Weaver said.

A few people pulled faces at that – me and Frankie included.

"So bearing in mind this historical theme, has anyone got any ideas for the float now?" Mrs Weaver said.

"Grannies," Frankie said under her breath.

Unfortunately, Mrs Weaver has ear radar of her own. "What was that, Francesca?" she asked, raising her eyebrows.

Frankie had to think quickly. "Er... grannies," she said. "We could all dress up as old grannies, and play bingo, and..."

"I don't think so, thank you, Francesca," Mrs Weaver said in her scariest no-nonsense voice. "Anyone else got any brilliant ideas?"

The M&Ms both smirked nastily at Frankie. Creeps! They're our enemies, if you didn't know. Emma Hughes and Emily Berryman, to be precise – but we don't like to waste our breath on their yucky names, so we call them the M&Ms instead. Ever seen *Star Wars*? I always expect that creepy Darth Vader music to start up whenever they walk into the room. One of these days, I swear

23

they're going to say to us, "Turn to the dark side, Sleepover Club!"

Emma put her hand up, all sickly-sweet smiles. "Miss, how about a tribute to all the famous people of Cuddington?" she said.

Mrs Weaver frowned. "Who were you thinking of, Emma?" she asked.

That stumped her! "Er... Well, my aunt was on Blind Date last year..." she said lamely.

All the boys – and all of us Sleepover girls, of course – started sniggering loudly. "Desperation and ugliness must run in the family," I said, loud enough for Emma to hear me. She went bright red and scowled at me. Ha! Got you back, Hughesy!

"We could do something about all the interesting sights of Cuddington," said Alan Baxter, class boffin. Like, *yeah*! 'Cos there are just *sooo* many, aren't there?

"That's a good idea, Alan," Mrs Weaver said, writing it up on the board. She was the only one who thought so, though, judging by the amount of people who were wrinkling up their noses in boredom. "Come on, the rest of you – use your brains!"

24

"Sport through the ages?" Simon Graham suggested. He's like me – a real sports nut.

I was just about to agree loudly with this idea – any excuse to dress up in my football kit! – when I heard an excited squeak come from next to me. Fliss!

"We could do... CLOTHES through the ages!" she burst out. "Fashion! What people wore a hundred years ago, right through to what people wear today!"

Everyone started shouting things out.

"Mini-skirts in the Sixties!"

"Flares in the Seventies!"

"Teddy boys!"

Even Mrs Weaver looked impressed by this. "I think that's a very good idea, Felicity," she said warmly. "Hands up if you agree."

A forest of hands shot up at once. A few boys' hands hung back – and I have to confess, I didn't put mine up STRAIGHT away, as I secretly fancied Simon's sports idea instead. But when Rosie gave me a fierce look, I decided I really should support Fliss. I'd never be forgiven otherwise.

Mrs Weaver was smiling now. I think she

was just relieved that someone had come up with something sensible. "Good thinking, Felicity," she said. "Everyone seems to like your idea."

Fliss blushed and looked down at her desk modestly, even though I knew that secretly she was practically wetting her pants with pride.

"Now, it's just about time for break," Mrs Weaver said, looking at her watch. "But keep thinking up ideas, everyone! I'll see what Mr Phillips thinks of 'fashion through the ages'. If he likes it, we'll start putting together materials for you to get working on tomorrow."

There was an excited buzz of chatter as we all went out into the playground. Fliss was beaming. Mrs Weaver often gets a bit impatient with her for day-dreaming or sneaking peeks in her little mirror to check her hair's OK all the time. But today she was the golden girl! And the thought of doing a whole project on her favourite thing – CLOTHES – was a dream come true.

As soon as we got outside, Frankie put her

hands on her hips and practically screamed, "So what's the news, Kenny? I've been dying to find out!"

I started to laugh. "You already HAVE found out, you nana. The carnival! That's what I was going to tell you about, but eager-beaver Weaver beat me to it."

Frankie's face fell. "Oh, phooey!" she moaned. "I thought it was going to be an idea for the next sleepover or something REALLY exciting."

"Talking of which..." Rosie said. "Anyone thought of anything?"

"Well, we've got to do some sort of carnival sleepover now," Lyndz said at once.

"Agreed!" I said. "If we have it at mine, we could use Molly the Monster as the bouncy castle!" Me and Molly – my middle sister – are about as friendly as Red Riding Hood and the big bad wolf.

"We could have a sort of hundred-years sleepover," Fliss said, chewing on her bottom lip thoughtfully.

Frankie felt Fliss's forehead, looking concerned. "Blimey, Fliss, that's two ideas you've had already this morning! No wonder you feel hot – your brain's probably about to explode!"

"And a hundred years is quite a long time for a sleepover, Fliss," I teased. "I don't think my mum and dad would be very keen on having us in the house for so long!"

"Yeah, do you fancy yourself as Sleeping Beauty or something?" Rosie quipped. "Falling asleep for a hundred years, only to be woken by a kiss from... Ryan Scott!"

Fliss tossed her long hair. "I didn't mean it has to LAST one hundred years, you derr-brains," she said scathingly as everyone else cracked up. "I meant, we could imagine what a sleepover would have been like one hundred years ago!"

"Like a 1901 sleepover?" Rosie said. Then she frowned. "I don't think they had telly then, though, did they?"

"What about sweets?" Lyndz asked anxiously.

"We had enough historical stuff when we stayed in that Blitz house," Frankie said with a shudder. "And there's no way I'm going without an inside toilet again, whatever you say!"

"Oh... Er... Well, we don't have to be that strict," Fliss said hurriedly. I could tell she didn't like the idea of not having a toilet either. "But maybe we could play old-fashioned games and eat old-fashioned sweets – like humbugs and toffee, that sort of thing – and maybe dress up, or... I don't know what they used to do in those days. Make love potions or something?"

Everyone pulled faces at the love potions idea. Fliss is the only one of us who's remotely interested in boys and lurve and all that soppy stuff.

"Is that your final answer?" I said in the end, leaning forward and shoving a pretend microphone under her nose.

"It's not a bad idea," Lyndz said, still sounding rather doubtful.

"Well, no-one's got any better ideas, have they?" Fliss pointed out. "So shall we do it?"

"Mmmm," "Yeah," "I suppose so," we all said at once – some of us less enthusiastically than others.

"Granny sleepover it is!" Frankie said with a wink.

CHAPTER THREE

The next day, we started work on our "fashion float". Mrs Weaver told us that the float would be divided up into ten sections – one for each decade. Our class was going to be split up into five groups. One group would work on the Fifties, one would do the Sixties, one the Seventies, and so on. In the meantime, Mr Phillips' class was going to work on the *first* five decades of the century.

"On the float, we want two people – a boy and a girl – representing each decade," Mrs Weaver said. "You can either just dress up in the typical fashion of that time, or you can dress up as a famous person from that decade. So, for example, if you were in the Sixties group, you could dress up in Sixties fashion – mini-skirts for example, or the hippy look. Or you could dress up as one of the Beatles, Neil Armstrong – you know, the first man on the moon, or... well, you get the idea."

"Do you think I'd look good in a mini-skirt?" Simon Graham shouted out, batting his eyelashes and making everyone giggle.

Mrs Weaver gave him one of her stern looks. "You'd look even better with your mouth closed, Simon," she said witheringly.

Then she split us up into groups of five or six people. Five people – perfect for the Sleepover Club! But then she said there had to be at least two boys and two girls in each group. Typical – boys always have to spoil everything.

In the end, we weren't TOO badly split up. Me and Frankie got to be in a group together, which was cool. We were with Simon, Neil and Maria Fonseca. I was pleased about that – at least we were guaranteed some laughs.

Rosie, Fliss and Lyndz were in a group with the twins, Alex and Joe Dunmore, who are pretty all right, too. At least Mrs Weaver hadn't put us with the M&Ms this time. She has a nasty habit of putting us in groups with them because she seems to think we'll make friends if we spend time together. In her dreams! I'd sooner be in a group with a man-eating crocodile and a dozen piranha fish, thanks!

Anyway, we were picked to do the Seventies' part of the float. Mrs Weaver handed round sheets with suggestions for famous people and events, and piles of library books she'd put together.

Our group started looking through some of the library books. "Look at those boots!" Frankie screeched, pointing at a picture excitedly. The soles were about six inches high and they were silver and glittery. "I want them!"

"Wow – punks!" Simon and Neil were saying. "Look – this one's got a safety pin through his cheek!"

"Glam rockers," Maria read aloud. "Look at

their trousers – they're so tight! And is that a wig he's wearing? That can't be his real hair!"

We all started snorting with laughter as we flicked our way through the rest of the books. There were lots of pictures of men wearing big, open-necked shirts with huge collars and gold medallions. "I wonder if our dads ever dressed like this?" I said, sniggering. "I know my mum used to have some gold hot-pants!"

"I wonder if Mrs Weaver ever dressed like THIS?" Simon whispered, holding up a picture of a punk girl with bright blue hair and three earrings in her nose.

That just set us all off in fits of giggles. The thought of a punk Mrs Weaver was totally crazy!

"I wouldn't mind dressing up as a glam rocker," Frankie said, once we'd all calmed down. "I just want to wear some of these funky boots! Unless one of you two fancy going on the float?"

I shook my head firmly. "I'm not dressing up in stoopid clothes," I said at once.

"Count me out," Maria said. "I'd break my

neck if I had to wear those things on my feet!"

Simon was quite keen to be Pele, the footballing star of the Seventies, but Maria and Frankie said they thought football was WAY too boring (as if!). In the end, Frankie persuaded him to be a punk by telling him they could dye his hair green with food colouring. "Wicked," he said, rubbing his hands together. "Mum'll KILL me!"

So that was that – one punk and one glam rocker. This was going to be *sooo* hilarious!

It was a humungously busy week. We had 'team meetings' on Wednesday and Friday morning to discuss our designs and give each other progress reports. Each team had to make some sort of sign or banner which said what their decade was. As all five of us were pretty useless at sewing, we went for a joint team effort to make a collage on card, rather than try anything with a needle and thread.

By the end of the week, it was starting to look pretty good. Maria had painted

The '70s in big purple letters in the middle, and Frankie had added silver glitter around the edges. Then we'd all brought in pictures of famous people and even some old photos of our mums and dads in outrageous Seventies gear!

Simon had brought in lots of pictures of footballers. Frankie had persuaded her mum to cut out pictures of pop stars from a collection of old magazines she had, and Neil had tracked down some pictures of old film stars. Me and Maria spent ages going through the library books, and made colour photocopies of all the weird Seventies fashions we could find. Our banner was starting to look truly faberoonie!

Fliss, Rosie and Lyndz had been hard at work, too. They were doing the Sixties, and Fliss – who else? – was going to be their 'model' on the float. Lyndz had found a great outfit for her in her mum's dressing-up box – a psychedelic swirly-patterned mini dress, knee boots and a wicked beehive wig.

"Loads of black eyeliner, and I'll be sorted," Fliss beamed. "One Sixties chick coming up!"

We were all glad for a break by the weekend. It was hard work being a designer. And what better way to let off some steam than with a sleepover?

"First things first," I said, once we'd all got back to my house and changed into our jeans. "Let's have some races around the garden. How about a three-legged race to kick off?"

But Fliss was shaking her head. "Kenny – Victorian girls wouldn't do that," she said solemnly. "They wouldn't do anything so undignified as tying their legs together and running around, getting all hot and sweaty!"

"Eh? Who said anything about Victorian girls?" I gawped. What was she on about?

Then it clicked. The 1901 sleepover! I'd completely forgotten!

"So what WOULD Victorian girls do?" Rosie asked. "Were they more into egg and spoon races instead?"

"No, they preferred swapping Pokémon cards," Frankie said. "So I've heard anyway..."

Fliss narrowed her eyes. "Don't be so silly! They did ladylike things!"

I felt my heart sink at that word – *ladylike*. It's one of the worst words in the English language.

Fliss started pulling scraps of material out of a bag, followed by lots of different coloured threads. "Here!" she beamed. "This is what Victorian girls used to do – sew samplers!"

"Samples of what?" Lyndz asked, frowning.

"No, SAMPLERS," Fliss said, passing us each a bit of material. "Like little tapestries. They'd sew things like Home Sweet Home on, or the alphabet. It was all the rage, in those days."

"Yeah, I bet," I said sarcastically. "Tapestry rage – I think I'm getting it already!"

"Those crazy Victorians sure knew how to have a good time," sniggered Rosie.

"Yeah, rock and roll," Frankie said.

Still, Fliss HAD gone to a lot of effort, getting all this stuff together, so...

"All right, all right," I said, with a sigh. "Pass us that blue thread, someone. One LCFC sampler coming up!"

Fliss bit her lip. "I don't think Victorian girls liked football," she started to say, but I gave her a murderous look and she quickly shut up. If I had to sew ANYTHING, I wanted to at least get something out of it – and a Leicester City Football Club sampler would look lovely above my bed!

My mum couldn't believe it when she found us five all sewing away in the garden. "Goodness! Have the bodysnatchers taken those noisy sleepover girls away and put some *young ladies* in their places?" she joked.

Just as she said that, I bashed my needle into my leg. "Ouch," I said, pulling it away. And then... "Oh no!" I wailed. "I've sewn my stupid tapestry to my T-shirt!"

"No, it's all right – it's still my clumsy daughter," Mum said, laughing.

"What do you think, ladies?" I said, getting up and jumping around, sending my tapestry flapping up and down. "I think it looks quite funky!"

We all started giggling at my awful attempt at a sampler, which was now firmly attached to my top. Typical me. I don't know WHY I was born a girl – I'd be much better at being a boy.

Luckily Mum had a good idea about what we could do next, once we explained why we'd been sewing in the first place. "How about croquet?" she said. "Your dad and I used to have a set – and that's a VERY old-fashioned game."

She dug the croquet out of the shed and put it up for us. Ever played croquet? It's quite a laugh, actually. You have these long wooden mallet things and the idea is to hit balls through hoops on the ground. It was all going quite well until Lyndz managed to get her foot stuck in a hoop and fall over, flat on her face!

"Ouch!" she wailed. "This is bad for your health, this game!"

"Oh, come on, you big girl's blouse," Frankie said – but just as she said it, she took a wild swing at a ball and managed to clobber her own leg with the mallet. "OW!" she yelled, hopping about clutching her battered leg. "I take it back, Lyndz – this IS a dangerous game!"

Me, Rosie and Fliss couldn't help giggling at the pair of them, all red-faced and cross. Oh, we're just *sooo* ladylike in the Sleepover Club, aren't we?

Then we sat on the grass and munched some liquorice that Fliss had brought along ("the proper old-fashioned stuff") while the invalids recovered.

"Sewing, croquet... what else can we injure ourselves with?" Rosie mused.

"How about making love potions?" Fliss said eagerly. "I've got an old recipe here..."

"NO!" we all said at once.

Fliss stuck her tongue out. "Well, WHAT, then?" she said. "Maybe we could write some poetry..."

The rest of us looked at each other in horror. This was getting worse and worse!

Then Lyndz glanced at her watch. "Er... well... *Neighbours* is about to start, actually," she said, looking a bit shame-faced.

"Definitely not!" Fliss said firmly. "Are we going to do this properly or not?"

I looked at Frankie. Frankie looked at Rosie and Rosie looked at Lyndz. "NOT!" we all shouted in the same breath.

Fliss looked disappointed as we all got up to go inside. "But..." she started.

"Oh, come on, Fliss," I said coaxingly. "Mum's got *Chicken Run* out on video for us as well, which I really want to see. And she's cooking sausages, chips and beans for tea – that's not very Victorian either..."

"Oh, all right," Fliss grumbled. "Back to the twenty-first century it is, then!"

"Phew," said Frankie. "And not a moment too soon!"

CHAPTER FOUR

Well, at least we TRIED to be old-fashioned and ladylike, didn't we? You can't say fairer than that. But at the end of the day, I guess we're all just too modern and twenty-first century to be anything else. You can't make a silk purse out of a sow's ear, as Frankie's gran would say!

The rest of the sleepover was more like the usual kind. We had our tea and watched the video, then went up to my bedroom.

I normally share a room with Molly the Monster but she was staying with one of her yucky mates for the night – goody! So we had the whole room to ourselves, without her telling us off for being noisy or mucking up her things. I keep telling Mum and Dad I need my own room – I've even asked them to build a wall in the middle of this one, so I don't have to see Molly's ugly mug first thing in the morning. But they're not having any of it.

We decided to play on my Playstation for a bit. I had this new game – Zombie Revenge – and before long, we were all hooked on it. It was really difficult to escape from the zombies – they'd grab your ankles when you were least expecting it, then suck your brains out through your ears. Grosserama!

"Hey, I've had an idea," Frankie said, after she'd been nobbled by the zombies for the tenth time in a row. "Why don't we have a SEVENTIES sleepover next time?"

"Yeah – excellent," I said at once, thinking back to all those hilarious library books. "We could have real fun dressing up – Afro wigs, flares, I'll borrow my mum's hot-pants, we can play loads of disco music..."

Fliss, Rosie and Lyndz were looking a bit put out. "Well, if we're going to have a

Seventies sleepover, we have to have a SIXTIES one too!" Rosie said. "Lyndz's mum has loads of cool dressing-up clothes we could use."

"And we could wear flowers in our hair," Fliss chimed in.

"Or we could have a space theme – you know, 'cos of man walking on the moon in 1969!" Frankie said excitedly.

"Sounds more fun than the 1901 sleepover," I said, and then caught sight of Fliss's expression. "Sorry, Fliss – it was a really good idea, but I just don't think it can have been much of a laugh, being around in those days."

"Wearing those long dresses and pinafores all the time," Frankie said with a shudder, patting her jeans thankfully.

"And doing all that girly stuff like sewing and playing the piano," Lyndz agreed. "Mind you, they did have to ride around on horses everywhere – that can't have been bad..."

"No cars – no telly – no Zombie Revenge," I said, shaking my head. "Poor, poor Victorians!"

* * *

The next week at school, Mrs Weaver sprung another surprise on us.

"Now, we're still going to have our float sessions on Friday mornings, where you can work on your banners and keep up to date with how everyone's getting on with the costume making," she said. "But I'm also going to start you off on another project connected with the carnival."

Everyone looked up hopefully at that.

"It's going to be a local history project," she said.

Doh!! Everyone looked down again and started muttering.

"Now, before you all start moaning and groaning, let me tell you a bit more about it," Mrs Weaver laughed. "I thought it would be a good idea to make a class book about where we live, and who lives here with us. We can call it Memories Of Cuddington, and I'll print a copy for everyone. What I want you to do is interview a grandparent who lives locally, or maybe an elderly neighbour if you have one, and ask them about their early memories of Cuddington. Then we can put everyone's interviews together in the book, and build up a picture of all the things that have happened here over the years."

"You mean, like the war, Miss?" brown-nosing Emily Berryman said.

"Yes, you can write about the Second World War, and how that affected people's lives if you want," said Mrs Weaver. "In fact, most of your grandparents were probably about your age when the war was on – think about that! Imagine what it was like growing up with all the men away, fighting abroad, while the women and children stayed at home, having stingy food rations to get by on, not knowing if their houses were going to be bombed at any moment..."

We all sat in silence for a moment. We'd done loads of stuff on the Blitz and that, but I'd never really thought about my grandparents being *kids* before. My Scottish grandparents I don't see that often, but my mum's parents live round the corner so we see them all the time. But as long as I've been around, Grandma and Grandad Littler have been... well, old, basically. The thought of them being young like us was weird.

"You'll be surprised how many interesting stories your grandparents will have," Mrs Weaver said. "If they grew up in wartime Britain, chances are they had it pretty tough. I think you'll all learn a lot from this project."

When teachers say things like "You'll learn a lot", it makes my heart sink right down into my trainers. My translation of that is – "You'll be bored a lot". But interviewing Grandma and Grandad wasn't exactly going to be loads of work. Hopefully I could get it over and done with in an hour or so – and it was a good excuse to eat lots of Grandma's yummy cakes at the same time. Hey, I know a good thing when I eat one...

Then Mrs Weaver took out a pile of papers. She'd photocopied lots of ancient editions of the *Leicester Mercury* which mentioned Cuddington in some way. As she passed them round, I suddenly remembered the old Victorian photographs of Cuddington she'd shown us for the millennium project and started to feel a bit more interested. It's quite freaky seeing such ancient pics of a place you know really well.

For a few minutes, we pored over the papers, "to get us in the mood" as Mrs Weaver said. Me and Frankie found a picture of Cuddington market from the Twenties, taken around May Day, showing all the festivities. There was this huge maypole in the market square, with loads of little kids dancing around it, holding on to ribbons. It was weird spotting some buildings we recognised in the background mixed up with some completely unfamiliar ones.

"Look – this butcher's shop is where the chemist is now," I said, pointing at it.

"Yeah, this old sweet shop has gone as well," Frankie said. "And this one. What does that say? Oh, it was a cobbler's. I wonder why they pulled down all these old buildings?"

"Oh wow!" I heard Lyndz say. She and Fliss had found a picture of King George VI – in Cuddington! "He was the Queen's dad, wasn't he?" Lyndz said, peering at it closely.

"Blimey – doesn't he look strict? You wouldn't want to muck about with him, would you?"

"Fancy the King of England coming to Cuddington!" Fliss marvelled.

"Yeah, if I was the king, I could think of a lot more interesting places to go," Frankie said.

"I think it was something to do with building the new road to Leicester," Lyndz said reading the article. "Hey – us Cuddington lot know how to show a king a good time, don't we?"

Rosie had found a dramatic picture. "Look at this!" she said, holding it up. "Fire sweeps Cuddington market – wow, look at the picture!"

We all gawped at the huge flames in the photo. They were so big, they'd spread through three or four buildings and were pouring out of the top windows.

"Hey, wait a minute," I said, grabbing the May Day picture. "Look! No wonder new buildings were put up in the market square. These old shops were burned down by the fire!"

"Ahh – a bit of detective work there, I see," Mrs Weaver said, standing behind me and looking at the pictures. "Well done, girls!"

Just then, there was a great shout of laughter from the back of the classroom. We all looked round to see what was going on.

Andy Taylor was holding up a picture and looking straight at me. "Hey, I didn't know you were THAT old, McKenzie!" he guffawed. "You hide your wrinkles well, don't you?"

"What are you on about, Andy-Pandy?" I said, going over to grab the picture off him. Stupid boy – probably one of his incredibly hilarious – not – tricks.

But as I looked at the photo, I gasped and did a real double-take. For there in the picture was... ME! I looked at the date on the newspaper and blinked in astonishment. 1945? Well, I certainly wasn't alive THEN!

The others crowded round. "Kenny, it's the absolute spit of you," Frankie declared, staring at the girl in the picture.

"I would swear that was you," Fliss said,

her mouth open wide. "I would even bet my Calvin Klein jeans that was you!"

The picture was of a parade through the centre of Cuddington. Children were carrying Union Jack flags and grinning at the camera. I – or rather, my double – was right at the front of the parade, holding up a flag with another girl.

"VE Day celebrations in Cuddington," Rosie read from the headline. "Right, so it was just after the war had ended."

"I always knew there was something weird about you," Frankie joked. "Go on, admit it – you're a time traveller and you can zip back and forwards between decades!"

"I can't believe McKenzie's got a double," Emma Hughes sniggered. "To think that TWO people in history have looked that gross!"

"Nature can be so cruel," Emily Berryman agreed.

I was too freaked out by the picture to react to the M&Ms, but I vowed I'd get them back later for it!

Even Mrs Weaver was a bit gobsmacked by the likeness. "Could this be a relative of yours, Laura?" she asked. "Do you have a grandmother or a great-aunt who was in Cuddington at this time?"

"Yeah, my grandma was," I said. "And people are always saying that I look like her..."

"What does the caption say under the picture?" Mrs Weaver said. "Does that help?"

"Violet Thompson and Rose Sanders lead the parade of schoolchildren through Cuddington market," I read. A huge grin was forming on my face. "And my grandma's name is Rose! It must be her!"

Mrs Weaver smiled at me. "Well, there you go!" she said. "I think your local history project has started already, Laura! Well spotted, Andy – more excellent detective work from my class. Now, didn't I say this project was going to be interesting?"

There was a rustle of papers as the rest of the class immediately started looking closer at the pictures – trying to find doubles of themselves, I guess!

I couldn't take my eyes off the picture of my grandma, looking about ten years old and smiling her head off. She looked really good fun – just the sort of person I could imagine myself getting on really well with. Now THAT was a funny thought. If we could somehow have met each other as kids then, would we have got on? Would we have liked each other?

Suddenly, I couldn't wait to go round and ask her all about it. Maybe this project wasn't going to be such a yawn after all!

CHAPTER FIVE

Mrs Weaver let me borrow the newspaper article and I took it round to Grandma's house that very evening. I'd showed it to Mum when I got home, and she was just as excited as me.

"Yes, Rose Sanders – that's Grandma all right," she said. "Sanders was her maiden name before she married Grandad. Goodness! Doesn't she look like you? People have said it to me before, but this really is a good likeness, isn't it?"

I was in such a rush to talk to Grandma, I didn't even change out of my school uniform.

That shows you how keen I was!

Grandma got all sentimental when she saw the picture. "Me and Vi Thompson! Who would have thought it?" she kept saying, shaking her head in disbelief. "Yes, I remember the parade very well. It was so exciting – war was over and I couldn't wait to see my daddy again. All the children got the day off school – remember, Bill?"

Grandad chuckled. "I do," he said, gazing into the distance. "I remember me and Harry Watling got told off for climbing up the stone cross in the market square. We had all these flags and bunting, you see, and we wanted to decorate everything in sight!"

"Was Grandad a bit of a wild one, then, Grandma?" I said, laughing.

"Ooh, he was that," she said mischievously. "Always getting in trouble with the local shopkeepers, I remember. And do you know what he was up to, the first time I ever clapped eyes on him?"

"What?" I asked, all agog.

She chuckled. "It was my first day at the grammar school, and the whole school was in the assembly hall," she said. "Mr Pickering – that was the headmaster, ooh, he was ever so strict – he suddenly started yelling at your grandad and his friend Harry for talking. Had them up in front of the whole school, he did, and rapped their knuckles with a ruler."

"Really?" I asked in delight. Funny how Grandad had never mentioned any of this to me before!

"Oh yes," Grandma said. "And I was eleven years old then and I remember nudging my friend Vi – her, in the picture – and the two of us giggling. Ooh, he was ever such a handsome lad, your grandad. I liked the look of him even then!"

"Wow," I said, trying to imagine the pair of them at grammar school together. "Hey, I should write all of this down," I said, suddenly remembering. "I've got to do a school project about grandparents growing up in Cuddington."

"Oh, well, I'm sure Grandma has lots more stories she can bend your ear with," Grandad said to me, pulling a naughty face behind Grandma's back. "Let's hope they aren't all about me getting into trouble at school, eh?"

But Grandma wasn't listening to him. She was staring at the picture of her and her friend Vi at the VE Day parade. "Ooh, Vi Thompson," she muttered to herself. "That lovely red hair of hers! She was ever such a pretty thing. A real looker, the boys used to say. I wonder what she's up to now?"

"Aren't you in touch with her any more?" I asked.

Grandma shook her head sadly. "No," she said. "We lost touch. Her dad came back from the war and then the whole family moved away. We sent Christmas cards and wrote the odd letter, but when you're twelve years old... You know, you make new friends and aren't very good at writing letters to old friends, are you?"

"And Grandma had started hanging around with all the boys at school then, anyway," Grandad teased.

Grandma rolled her eyes at me. "Yes – that's true, I'd met your grandad then, and it was downhill from then on!" she said.

I asked them a few more questions about growing up in Cuddington and how it had changed over the years, before Mum rang up with a message for me to come home for my tea.

Grandma reluctantly gave me the newspaper clipping back, and I promised I'd get a copy made of it for her. Suddenly her eyes had gone all far-away, as if she was lost in the past.

As I cycled back home, I found myself wondering how I'd feel if, years and years into the future, my granddaughter showed me an old picture of me and Frankie together. How would I feel if we'd lost touch? It would bring back *sooo* many memories of all the mad things we'd done together. No wonder Grandma had looked so sentimental at the sight of her old friend.

And that's when I had one of my fantastic ideas. Now you know me – I'm always coming up with some stuff for us to get our teeth into. But this one was a real corker! What if I could somehow get hold of this Violet Thompson and organise a reunion for her and Grandma? Now, just how cool would that be? And what an amazing history project it would be as well! Top marks for Ms McKenzie, I reckon!

When I told Mum my idea, she immediately wanted to help out. "Let's look through the phone book," she suggested, passing it over to me. "What was her surname? Thompson?"

"Yeah," I said doubtfully, "but she'll have changed her name if she got married. Everyone did in those days, didn't they?"

"That's true," said Mum. "But you never know – perhaps she never married."

"But maybe she doesn't live in this area," I pointed out. "Grandma did say she'd moved away, remember."

Mum tutted. "Kenny – you'll never find her with that attitude," she scolded. "Think positive!"

Just then, I found all the Thompsons in the phone book. There was absolutely stacks of them – practically a whole page!

"Any V. Thompsons there?" Mum asked, craning over my shoulder. "No – not a sausage.

Well, at least it's saved you a few phone calls! And before you ask – no, you can't ring every one of those Thompsons up and ask them. The phone bill would be astronomical!"

I closed the phone book and slumped back in my chair. What now?

"I suppose I could look in the library at the weekend," I said.

"Yes," Mum said. "Good idea. Or you could try asking the grammar school to see if they still keep old records of all their pupils. You never know, there might be a forwarding address there somewhere."

"Mmmmm." I flicked idly through the phone book. "Hey, I wonder if she has any brothers who might be listed here?" I said, trying to 'think positive'. "Because they would be Thompsons still, wouldn't they?"

"Very true," said Mum. "Smart thinking, Batman!"

"I'll ask Grandad," I said. "You never know – Vi may have had an older brother who was closer to Grandad's age." I smiled to myself. I was going to enjoy this little bit of detective work! Then I remembered Mum's love of gossip. "By the way, don't tell Grandma about any of this, will you?" I said. "I want it to be a *biiig* surprise."

"Right you are," Mum said. "Mum's the word!"

"Not this time," I giggled, "GRANDMA's the word!"

The rest of the Sleepover Club were as interested in my project as I was. "Awesome!" breathed Frankie when I'd finished telling them about it. "That's so exciting! Much better than my interview with Mrs Millard next door. All she could talk about was how cheap everything used to be, and how children had better manners in those days. I mean – that's going to be a fascinating interview when I write it up, isn't it?"

"That's so cool about your grandma," Rosie said. "Oh, I hope we can track Vi down! Imagine how nice it will be for them both."

"I know," I said. "I keep thinking, say we all lose touch in the future, what it would be like for one of our grandchildren to reunite us. Wouldn't it be fab?"

"Oh, but we're not going to lose touch!" Lyndz said at once. "I don't even want to think about that – it would be awful!"

Fliss started giggling. "I wonder what we're all going to look like when we're grannies?" she said. "I hope I don't have too many wrinkles!"

"Kenny will still be wearing a track suit and trainers," Frankie said. "And she'll be bullying her grandchildren into having a kick-around with her in the park!"

"Lyndz will still be riding horses," Rosie added. "She'll probably have a whole riding school of her own by then!"

"Oh, I hope so!" Lyndz said wistfully. "And all your grandchildren can have free lessons – management's orders!"

We all cracked up at Lyndz's earnest face.

"Seriously, though," I said, "has anyone got any bright ideas about finding Vi? I managed to get Grandad on his own the other night but he couldn't help much more. He said he thought Vi had an older brother called Arthur but he wasn't sure. I can't ask Grandma, it would just spoil the surprise."

"So have you looked in the phone book under A. Thompson?" Frankie said.

"Yes," I sighed. "And there are *loads* of them. I started ringing some of them up until Mum caught me and told me off. She said if I wanted to make lots of calls, I could pay for them out of my pocket money. And as I owe all my next month's pocket money to Dad for breaking the TV remote control..." I shrugged. I never seem to have any pocket money – every time I've just about paid off one debt, I go and break something else and have to pay for *that*.

"We could all chip in for the calls," generous Lyndz offered at once.

"Speak for yourself," Frankie said. "I'm skint!"

"So am I," Rosie said.

"And it's my mum's birthday soon and I'm desperately trying to save up enough for some Chanel nail varnish she wants," Fliss said.

I bit my lip to stop myself giggling at Fliss's solemn face. "Oh, I wouldn't dream of depriving your mum of her nail varnish," I said to her. "No, we'll just have to think of something else. How about if we go to the library on Saturday morning and see if we can find anything there?"

"Agreed!" the others said.

"Vi – we're coming for you," Frankie said solemnly. "Ready or not!"

CHAPTER SIX

Before we could do any of that, we had Friday's sleepover to look forward to! It was a Sixties theme this time. We'd decided to have it at Lyndz's house, as she has the most *awesome* box of dressing-up clothes. Now, you know me – I'm really not into clothes, and would be quite happy to wear the same tracksuit or pair of jeans every day for the rest of my life. But even *I* think the dressing-up box is fab, so you can imagine what heaven it is for the others!

Me and Frankie had left the other three to organise everything, promising that we would take full responsibility for the next sleepover – the Seventies one. So all Friday, Lyndz, Fliss and Rosie kept going into a huddle and whispering their plans to each other. By the end of school that day, I was ready to burst, I wanted to know what they were up to so badly!

Lyndz lives a little way out of Cuddington, so her dad picked us up after school. As soon as we got in the car, he immediately started blasting out some weird music.

"If you're going to San Francisco..." this bloke warbled, "be sure to wear some flowers in your hair..."

We all cracked up at that. "Dad, what's this rubbish?" Lyndz spluttered.

We could see her dad grinning in his mirror. "This is real Sixties music, this," he said. "Flower power! Everyone stripped off and painted themselves, and put flowers in their hair in those days!"

"What, you as well, Mr Collins?" Frankie asked cheekily.

"Me? No, love, I was only about ten in the summer of love – that was 1967," he told us.

"But I remember my big brother growing his hair long and painting flowers on his face." He chuckled. "I don't mind telling you, he looked a right ninny and all!"

"Who? Uncle Lawrence?" Lyndz asked, bouncing up and down on her seat with laughter. "I can't believe it! He is so stiff these days!"

"Well, he wasn't in the Sixties, believe me," Lyndz's dad said with a chuckle. "You should have seen his clothes! He had these big purple velvet flares, bell-bottoms they were called, and this long sheepskin coat that he practically lived in. God, it stank something rotten!"

Fliss wrinkled up her nose in horror. Flissy would rather DIE than wear smelly clothes!

"So, Mr C, do you remember when Neil Armstrong first stepped on the moon?" space-nerd Frankie asked eagerly.

The rest of us groaned. Sometimes Frankie is dead predictable. But Lyndz's dad seemed just as enthusiastic as she was.

"Remember?" he said, slapping the steering wheel excitedly. "Do I ever! The whole country stopped to watch the news on TV! The whole country! And suddenly every kid my age wanted to be an astronaut and see the moon for themselves!" He shook his head, remembering it all. "I know I did. Me and Jack Baker from next door poured his mum's goldfish out of the goldfish bowl so we could take turns wearing it on our heads!"

The rest of us giggled, but Lyndz looked appalled. "And what happened to the goldfish?" she asked sternly. "I hope you put it in water!"

That made us laugh even more. Trust Lyndz to think of the goldfish first!

By the time we got to Lyndz's house, her dad had really got us in a giggly mood with all his funny stories. But even so, it was a relief to get out of the car and away from all that warbling hippy music.

"Hello, girls," Mrs Collins said as we all piled into the house. "What will it be first – dressing-up box or some home-made biscuits?"

"Oooh – BISCUITS!" we all said at the same time. Lyndz's mum is a fab cook, and seems to be extra-good at making biscuits that melt in your mouth. Even Fliss tucks in, and she's super health-conscious about fattening things.

This time, Mrs Collins made the most colourful biscuits I'd ever seen. Each one had a rainbow of jelly tots and hundreds and thousands over it. She'd even put food colouring in some to make them pink, yellow and blue!

"I was only a little girl in the Sixties, but I do remember how colourful it was," she explained. "All the teenage girls on our street wore the tiniest mini-skirts, in colours so bright they hurt your eyes. My neighbours drove a Mini – with rainbows painted all over it. My mum and dad used to call it an eyesore, but I thought it was the most gorgeous car I'd ever clapped eyes on."

I was secretly starting to think that everyone had gone a bit bonkers in the Sixties. I crammed another biscuit in my mouth and looked expectantly at Lyndz, Fliss and Rosie. "So what have you Sixties chicks got planned for us tonight, then?" I asked.

"Dressing up and face painting," Lyndz said at once.

"A space-race game," Rosie added.

"And a Sixties sing-along," Fliss said mysteriously.

"Sounds cool!" I said. "Lead me to my velvet flares!"

The dressing-up box was even fuller than usual. Lyndz told us her mum had gone on a charity shop spree when she'd heard about the Sixties sleepover, and had come up trumps with some totally incredible outfits.

"Look at this dress!" Fliss squealed, pulling out a hot pink stretchy mini-dress. There was a gap between the top and bottom halves of the dress, linked only by big silver rings. "Is that funky or what?" she said, throwing off her school clothes at once and scrambling into it.

"More like obscene," Frankie said. "It's so short, we can practically see your knickers."

"I think they liked to show a lot of flesh in the Sixties," Lyndz said, holding up a bright orange mini-skirt she'd found. "I mean, this is more of a BELT than a skirt."

"Hey, hey, hey!" I said, pulling out some enormous trousers. They were a pastel pink colour with silver bells hanging from the bottom and flares so big you could hide a small dog up each leg. "Check these babies out!"

The others snorted with laughter as I put them on and started prancing around. "Someone must have actually gone into a shop and paid good money for these when they were new," I marvelled. "How mad is that?"

By now, we'd all found something funny to wear. Frankie had a pair of denim hipsters and this beaded waistcoat which jingled every time she moved. Fliss had her pink dress. Lyndz passed on the orange mini-skirt – she's got this *stoopid* idea in her head that she's fat, but she's not at all. Instead, she went for this long dress that was as big as a tent, with psychedelic swirls and bits of mirror all over it. I had my pink flares and found a purple crocheted top to go with them, and Rosie chose a long white dress with PEACE painted on it, and a bright orange headband with feathers sticking out. "Just call me Pocohontas," she said, giggling.

"Now the face paints," Lyndz announced, pulling out a couple of sets. "Who wants me to do them?"

That was the point where things *really* started to get silly. After we'd all made each other up, we were in shrieks of laughter. Frankie painted a big eye in the middle of my forehead, and I painted flowers on her cheeks and neck. Lyndz gave Rosie a heart on one cheek and a daisy on the other, Rosie painted multi-coloured rainbows above Fliss's eyes, and Fliss wrote LOVE on Lyndz's forehead. I laughed so much, the others said that the eye on my forehead looked like it was winking!

"OK, I dare us to go out like this and see what people say," Frankie suddenly said, with the old familiar glint in her eye.

"What – out in the streets, like this?" Fliss said.

"No – out on the moon, what do you think?" Frankie said. "Of course I mean out on the streets! C'mon, it'll be hilarious!"

"We can go to the sweet shop down the road," I said, warming to the idea. "We can just breeze in as if everything's normal – and check out the looks they give us in there!"

"I'm up for it," Rosie said. "And we do need some sweets, don't we?"

"What do you reckon, Fliss?" Lyndz asked.

"What if someone from school sees us?" Fliss said anxiously.

"If you mean Ryan Scott, he lives miles away from here," Lyndz reminded her. "In fact, none of the boys in our class live anywhere near here – so you're safe!"

"OK, then," Fliss said in the end. I should have guessed that that was what she'd been so worried about. Fliss hates the idea of anyone she knows seeing her do something stupid and 'uncool'. Luckily, the rest of us have no such probs about acting stupidly any time, any place, in front of anyone!

Before we left, we paraded up and down in front of Lyndz's family, giving them a bit of a fashion show. Lyndz's parents clapped and cheered, but Tom, one of Lyndz's older brothers, laughed until he was nearly crying.

"I've got to get a photo of this," he said, grabbing a camera. "I can use it for my school art project!"

"No way!" said Fliss at once.

"What's your project on?" I asked curiously.

"Beautiful women in fashion," he said, fiddling with the shutter.

Fliss beamed at that, and tossed her hair over her shoulder. "Oh – I suppose so, then," she said.

CLICK! CLICK! CLICK!

"What's your project REALLY about?" I asked, once he'd taken a few photos. There was no WAY Tom was really doing a project on fashion!

"My freaky family," he grinned. "And that's going to be perfect material for a collage of Lyndz and her freaky mates!"

Tom and his dad burst out laughing. Lyndz's mum looked as if she was trying her hardest not to laugh, too.

"Tom!" Lyndz squealed. "That is *sooo* sneaky!"

Fliss had gone a funny purple colour and

74

looked absolutely mortified at the thought of appearing in Tom's project.

"Come on, let's go and scare some people on the streets," Rosie said hurriedly.

"Yeah, before I kill my horrible brother!" Lyndz fumed. "I'll get you back for this one, you pig!"

We could hear them all chuckling even after we'd shut the front door. I had to admit, it WAS pretty funny. What was Tom's art teacher going to think when he saw the pictures? Despite the fact that he'd played such a rotten trick on us, I couldn't help my lips twitching – and then I couldn't help this huge laugh bursting out of me. "Sorry!" I gasped. "But it is quite f-f-funny!"

"His teacher's going to think we're complete freaks," Lyndz said, starting to laugh, too. "He'll probably get top marks because the teacher feels sorry for him!"

"Beautiful women in fashion – that was inspired," Rosie giggled. "He must think we're totally vain to fall for that one!"

In the end, even Fliss saw the funny side – just! By the time we got to the sweet shop,

we were all breathless with giggles. "Rosie –
you're the best actress," Frankie said. "If you
can pull this off with a straight face, I'll buy
you a Flake."

Rosie grinned and took a few deep
breaths. "Come on, then," she said, and we
followed her into the shop.

Rosie IS a pretty good actress, actually.
She has this amazing poker face that means
she can get away with the most outrageous
fibs. She's one of those people you never
know whether to believe or not. And this
time she played a blinder.

"Wow, man," she drawled at the counter,
staring up at the jars of brightly coloured
sweets. "Those colours are just bee-yew-tee-
ful. Totally far-out!"

Lyndz was already bright red, trying not to
explode with giggles, and Frankie had stuffed
her purse into her mouth to try and stop
herself from roaring out loud. But Rosie was
on a roll.

"Groovy, baby," she said dreamily to Mrs
Coombs, the shopkeeper. "Do you have any
of those cosmic cola bottles?"

"Cosmic...? Eh? Are you taking the mickey?" Mrs Coombs asked sharply.

"Mickey? That's a beautiful name," Rosie said, waving her hands in the air, with a serene smile on her face. "No, my name is Lovechild. I come in peace."

We all just cracked up at that. Lyndz lost it so badly, she gave herself hiccups.

"Lyndsey Collins, is that you with all that muck on your face?" Mrs Coombs asked.

HIC! was all Lyndz could say to that.

"I don't know what you're playing at, but if you want any sweets, you're going to have to stop this nonsense right away!" Mrs Coombs said crossly, folding her arms across her chest.

Rosie came out of character straight away. "Sorry – we're just practising for the school play," she said with a charming smile. "Hippies On The Run, it's called."

"Humph!" Mrs Coombs said, not believing a word of it. "Well, you can all just run out of this shop again, if you're going to play silly beggars with me!"

We all stopped laughing at once, and put

our orders for sweets in quickly while we still had a chance of being served. A sleepover without sweets was just unthinkable!

Outside the shop again, we all leaned against the wall, breathless with giggles. "Rosie, you were fantastic," Frankie said, handing over her Flake.

"Top banana!" I agreed.

"She's never going to serve me again!" Lyndz wailed, her lips twitching with laughter. "She thinks we're completely mad!"

"She's right," Fliss moaned. "You ARE all completely mad! Now quick – let's get home before anyone else sees us!"

CHAPTER SEVEN

The rest of the sleepover was just as much fun. Lyndz and Rosie had put together this 'space race' game, where we were timed running round the garden, collecting silly things to build a rocket with. You had to pick up a plank of wood, a roll of Sellotape, a thermos flask, a plastic telescope and a cardboard box, then put on Lyndz's dad's white overalls (nearest they could get to a space suit) and moonwalk to the end of the garden, arms still full of stuff. It was such a stupidly funny game, we ended up playing it about three times over, getting more and more breathless each time.

For the last round, Frankie made up an 'asteroid' variation where everyone else could throw ping-pong balls (oops – I mean asteroids) at the astronaut, who had to dodge them, or lose points. It was really hard trying to carry everything and still duck from the hail of asteroids – and it was even funnier to watch!

After that, we all felt really tired and hungry, and we wolfed down our tea in no time. Fliss had brought along a tape of Sixties music that her step-dad Andy had put together, so after tea, we had a bit of a Sixties disco in Lyndz's bedroom, working out some really wild dance routines.

All in all, we agreed that the Sixties was a pretty cool decade – a lot better than the Victorian sleepover we'd had anyway. As Lovechild – alias Rosie – might have said, it was totally groovy, man!

On Saturday morning, we started the search for Vi Thompson with a trip to Cuddington library. I told the lady at the reception desk that we were trying to trace someone who'd lived here over fifty years ago, and she showed us the local reference section on the computer which had a database of thousands of names.

I felt really excited as I typed 'Violet Thompson' and hit the return button – but nothing came up at all. Great! That was a good start! Then I typed in 'Arthur Thompson' and hit return. I wasn't really expecting anything. I mean, if Vi wasn't on the list, why would her brother be? But just to prove me wrong, a few names came up on the screen.

"Yippee! Thompson, Arthur, 1928-1997," I read aloud. "Oh. Well, the first one is already dead. That's not much use to us."

"The second one was born in 1940," Frankie said. "So he's too young."

"How about the next one – born 1932? That would be about right, wouldn't it?" Rosie said.

We all started trying to work out the maths. "So he'd have been thirteen when the war ended..." Lyndz said, frowning.

"... And Grandma was about eleven in the newspaper photo," I said. "So, yeah, this

Arthur Thompson could have been Vi's big brother."

We scanned through the rest of the list, but the other Arthur Thompsons were either all too old or too young.

"One Arthur Thompson, there's only one Arthur Thompson," Frankie sang tunelessly.

"Well, one Arthur Thompson is a start," Fliss said. "So how do we find out more details about him?"

I double-clicked on his name and the screen changed.

NAME: THOMPSON, ARTHUR JOHN

BORN: 13/1/32

SCHOOL: NOT KNOWN

OCCUPATION: NOT KNOWN

PLACE OF BIRTH: KING GEORGE'S HOSPITAL, LEICESTER

LAST KNOWN ADDRESS: 35, MILTON ROAD, CUDDINGTON

"Yahoo! An address!" I squealed.

"Milton Road, where's that?" Rosie said. "Quick, someone get the Cuddington street map!"

Frankie grabbed it and the five of us pored over it. "Here," Lyndz said at last, stabbing a finger on to the map. "It's not far from the canal. We could cycle over there this afternoon."

"Let's do it," I said, grinning with excitement. This was all turning out to be a lot easier than I'd thought!

Still, you know what they say about counting your chickens before they've hatched. I should have known the 'find Vi' plan was all going a bit too smoothly.

The five of us met up after lunch with our bikes, and cycled over to Milton Road. The others waited at the gate while I went up to the front door and rang the bell.

A woman answered, clutching a red-faced baby in her arms. Somewhere behind her, another child was wailing loudly.

"Yes?" the woman answered, jiggling the grizzling baby up and down on her hip. "What is it?"

"I'm looking for a Mr Arthur Thompson," I said in my most polite voice. "The computer at the library says he lives here."

"Well, he doesn't," she said flatly. "WE live here – and have done for the last two years, so..."

She started to shut the door, but I couldn't leave it there. "Do you know if a Mr Thompson lived here before that?" I tried quickly, before the door slammed in my face.

I could tell she really wasn't interested. "Sorry, darling, no," she said. "Is that all? Only I'm a bit busy right now."

"Yes," I said, feeling hugely disappointed. "Thank you. Sorry to bother you."

I made the thumbs-down sign to the others as I walked back to the gate. Now what? We were back to square one!

We walked our bikes back into the village, all feeling a bit dejected. I was racking my brains furiously, trying to come up with another approach. "Do you think any of your grandparents might know something?" I asked the others in the end. I was starting to feel desperate now that the trail had gone cold.

"None of mine have ever lived around here," Frankie said. "Sorry."

"Nor mine," Lyndz said.

"My grandparents are too young," Fliss said, looking doubtful. "The ones on my mum's side, anyway. I'll ask if you like, but I don't reckon they'll be much help. And I never see my grandparents on my dad's side."

"Rosie?" I said. "Your granny and grandpa live in Cuddington, don't they?"

"Ye-e-e-es," she said slowly. "But I hardly ever see them. They're my dad's parents and Mum's fallen out with them."

"What about *her* parents?" I asked, feeling increasingly desperate.

"They're both dead," Rosie said, and shrugged. "I mean, I'll ask Granny if you really want me to but... I don't want to upset my mum, that's all."

"Oh, please, Rosie! Please, please, please, on bended knees!" I said, sinking to my knees in the middle of the street.

She stopped looking so solemn then, and giggled. "All right, you nutter!" she said. "Leave it with me – I'll see what I can do."

I don't know about you, but I hate not

being able to get what I want when I want it! Oh, don't get me wrong, I'm not a spoiled brat who always gets my own way or anything. But with this Vi-hunt, I was starting to get really wound up, not being able to get an immediate result. It would all be so fantastic reuniting Grandma and Vi – I HAD to get hold of her somehow!

Luckily, we were so busy at school with our work on the float, I was able to forget Project Vi for a bit. On the Wednesday and Friday, we worked really hard on our banner, and between us, we slowly put together a good collection of clothes and make-up for our models.

Maria had trawled the charity shops and found a pair of stack-heeled knee-high boots for Frankie – who customised them with silver glitter! My mum had lent Frankie her shiny gold hot-pants on the condition that we didn't tell too many people where they'd come from, and we'd borrowed a pink T-shirt from Lyndz's dressing up box with *Charlie's Angels* written on it, which was a big Seventies TV programme. To top it off,

Frankie's mum had found a Tina Turner-style wig at a jumble sale for 50p. Frankie was a bit squeamish about wearing a second-hand wig, but once she put it on, we all shrieked with laughter and INSISTED that she wore it on the float!

So that was our 'glam rocker' sorted. Now there was just the punk to kit out. Simon was still up for having his blonde hair done into green spikes, with Frankie's food-colouring idea. He'd tie-dyed an old T-shirt and ripped holes in it until it looked properly scuzzy and punky. Neil had borrowed a pair of leather trousers from his brother, and Simon's mum had picked up a black leather jacket from – you guessed it – another charity shop, which Simon and Neil had punked up brilliantly with silver studs and chains on the back. To put the cherry on the cake, Maria had lent Simon her dog's black studded collar to wear around his neck!

The others seemed to be getting on pretty well, too. Fliss's big dilemma was how to do her hair – big 'beehive' style, all piled up on her head, or two long plaits for the hippy look. Rosie was trying to talk her into cutting it all off into a chic bob, but Fliss wasn't having any of it.

And Lyndz was pleased as anything, too – Mrs Weaver had asked for volunteers to walk in front of the float with buckets full of sweets, throwing them to the crowds. A dream job for sweet-tooth Collins anyway, but then one morning, she burst into the classroom, all smiles.

"I've had the best brainwave of my life!" she told us excitedly.

"What?" we all said at once.

Mrs Weaver came into the classroom, so Lyndz just shook her head and smiled mysteriously. She even did that annoying thing where she tapped the side of her nose – don't you just hate it when people do that?

Luckily, we didn't have too long to wait to find out what she was plotting. As soon as Mrs Weaver started talking about the carnival, Lyndz put her hand up in the air and waved it about importantly.

"Yes, Lyndsey?" Mrs Weaver asked.

"Mrs Weaver, you know I'm going to be

one of the sweet throwers at the carnival?" Lyndz said, going a bit pink as everyone looked at her.

"Yes?" Mrs Weaver said.

"Well, I was wondering if I could ride Alfie in front of the float while I throw out the sweets," she said in a rush. "Oh – Alfie's a horse, by the way. He's ever so good, he wouldn't be any trouble."

Mrs Weaver raised her eyebrows at Lyndz's suggestion, but then she smiled. "That's a great idea!" she said warmly. "As long as your riding school will let you borrow him for the day, of course. And providing he won't be scared of all the crowds – there are going to be lots of people and loud music there, remember."

Lyndz shook her head at once. "Oh, no, he's been to lots of festivals and shows and things before. He's never been frightened of anything like that," she said confidently. "I'll phone the riding school tonight to see if it's OK!"

I nudged Lyndz as Mrs Weaver started talking about something else. "Nice one!" I whispered.

She grinned happily, and I knew that Lyndz would enjoy the carnival even more if she could share it with her beloved Alfie.

Sure enough, Mrs McAllister said it was fine for Alfie to accompany Lyndz to the carnival – providing he wore a 'McAllister's Riding School' banner to give them some free advertising!

Even though the week was really good fun, I was getting more and more antsy about my local history project. Time was running out. I only had another week to find Vi. After that, the carnival was going to begin, with or without my planned reunion. I had to get on the case and find her – fast!

CHAPTER EIGHT

The next big event in our diaries was the Seventies sleepover, organised by Frankie and yours truly. This time, we were going to have it at Frankie's house. Frankie is my oldest friend in the world – we met at playgroup, before we'd even started school, so I know her parents really well, too. They're ace – really funny and nice. Going there is like being at my second home, only there's no annoying big sisters to wind me up – just Frankie's cute baby sister, Izzy, who's a lot easier to handle!

At lunch time on the Thursday before the

sleepover, me and Frankie went to eat our sandwiches on our own, so we could make a few secret plans. We had to make our sleepover at least as good as the Sixties one, after all!

On the way back to Frankie's on Friday night, Lyndz swung her bag and grinned at the rest of us. "I've got a surpri-ise in here," she sang. "And I'm not saying what it i-is until we get to Frankie's!"

"I've got a surprise too," Rosie said, wiggling her eyebrows up and down at us. "And I'm not telling either."

"Well, me and Frankie have got LOADS of surprises for tonight, so nerrr!" I said quickly, not wanting to be left out.

"Yeah, but you're MEANT to have surprises – you've organised the sleepover," Lyndz pointed out. "Whereas my surprise is the real McCoy!"

"It's not going to be much of a surprise now that you've told us you've got a surprise," Frankie said.

"Mine's better anyway," Rosie said mysteriously.

Fliss was looking a bit left out. "No-one SAID we all had to bring surprises, or I would have brought one too," she said crossly.

"Don't worry, Fliss, your sparkling wit and intellectual conversation is enough for us," I said, grinning at her. "Who could ask for anything more?"

She looked at me uncertainly, not sure if I was joking or not. Luckily we'd got to Frankie's house by then anyway, and everyone was taking their shoes off and cooing over baby Izzy and saying hello to Frankie's mum.

After we'd changed out of our school uniforms and had a quick drink, we went out into the garden to play our first game – the dressing-up race! First of all, you had to pull on some mega-tight trousers and Frankie's silver carnival boots as fast as you could, then run two lengths of the garden, then grab a pogo stick we'd borrowed (pogo sticks were way big in the Seventies, apparently) and try to pogo your way to the finish line.

"You lose points for breaking your neck or

falling off the boots," Frankie announced, "and you're totally disqualified if you break the boots themselves!"

"Could we use these at all?" Lyndz said, pulling her 'surprise' out of her bag. We all burst out laughing when we saw what she'd brought – three Afro wigs! "Mum said that disco music was really big in the Seventies," she explained, "and loads of people had hair like this!"

"Wicked!" I said, pulling a wig on at once. "How do I look?"

"Like a complete prat!" Rosie said, giggling. "I know – you have to wear a wig while you pogo – and if you pogo so hard your wig falls off, you have to go back to the start."

"Agreed!" we all said.

Have you ever been on a pogo stick? It is really hard – even if you've got quite a good sense of balance. Basically, it's a long stick with a rubbery bottom and two steps for your feet about twenty centimetres up. You're meant to bounce along, without letting your feet touch the floor. Easier said than done, believe me!

While we all managed to run up and down in skin-tight can't-breathe trousers and huge stack-heeled boots without too many injuries (and, more importantly, no damage to Frankie's precious silver boots), none of us could manage more than a few bounces on the pogo stick before wobbling off and crashing to the ground.

"I declare the pogo a no-go," Frankie said breathlessly after we'd all bruised ourselves enough times with some spectacular falls. "Those Seventies kids must have all been circus freaks if they managed to work these things."

"What's next, then?" Fliss asked as we all lay on the grass, sucking sherbet lemons.

"Maybe we should have my surprise next," Rosie said.

"Go for it," I said, rubbing a bump on my knee which was rapidly going a nasty purple colour.

"Brilliant – I've been dying to tell you this all day," she said, sitting up. "Well, I went over to my granny and grandpa's last night…"

I immediately sat bolt upright too, practically fizzing with excitement. "Oh, what? What have you found out?" I said.

Rosie smiled. "It was really nice to see them actually," she said. "You know I'd been a bit worried about going because I hadn't seen them for ages, and I didn't want my mum to take it the wrong way, and..."

"Yeah, so was she all right about it?" Lyndz asked.

"She was fine!" Rosie said. "She was totally cool about it, which was a real relief, because—"

"Oh, what did you find out?" I asked impatiently. "Sorry – but I just want to know! Don't make me wait any longer!"

"Make her wait, Rosie – you take your time!" Frankie shouted to wind me up.

"Yeah, take as long as you want," Fliss said. "In fact, tell us every single detail about the visit first!"

Rosie took one look at my face and laughed. "I think there will be an exploding McKenzie any second if I don't get on with it," she said. "All right, Kenz, I'll put you out of your misery." She crunched through the rest of her boiled sweet. "Well, my granny's a bit too young to remember much about the war, but my grandpa is about the same age as yours is, Kenny – in fact, he remembered your grandad from school, said he was always getting into trouble."

"That would be right," Frankie said. "Kenny's definitely a chip off the old block."

"Yeah, go on," I said encouragingly.

"There's more," she said, enjoying her moment. "So I asked him if he remembered Violet or Arthur Thompson as well."

"And?" I burst out.

"Well, he didn't remember them from school," Rosie said, "but—"

I couldn't help it – this huge groan came out of me. "Oh no!" I wailed.

"BUT," Rosie said loudly, "he said the name definitely rang a bell. 'Arthur Thompson – where do I know that name from?' he kept saying, over and over again."

The others had all sat up in interest now. You had to hand it to Rosie – she was a good storyteller. If it had been me, I'd have blurted the basic facts out straight away, but here she was, with the rest of us hanging on her every word.

"In the end, I just got on with the interview for the history project," Rosie said. "And then suddenly, just as I was asking him about rationing during the war, he slapped his leg so hard, the sofa practically shook. 'Got it!' he shouted. 'He played cricket with us every Sunday – red-haired lad, was he?' 'Well, his sister had red hair,' I said, 'so that would make sense.'"

"So he knew Arthur!" I shouted. "What else did he say?"

"Well, once he'd remembered that, he suddenly remembered loads more," Rosie went on. "Said he was the best spin bowler Cuddington had ever seen, and all this. But then came the real clincher..."

We all just stared at her, waiting for the rest. Even I didn't say anything this time!

"I told him that your gran had said the family had moved away just after the war," she said. "I just wanted to check that he'd definitely got the right bloke – because I wondered how come my grandad would be playing cricket with him if they didn't live in the area any more. Anyone mind if I have the last jelly baby?"

"No!" we all said at once. Anything to keep her going!

"Cheers," she said, popping it into her mouth. "'Yes, they DID move away, didn't they?' he says. 'But only to Leicester – they still kept the fruit and veg stall going in Leicester market.' 'WHAT fruit and veg stall?' I say. 'Thompsons' fruit and veg – they've had the stall in the family for donkey's years!' he says. *'And there's probably still a Thompson running it to this day!'*"

Rosie's face was a picture of triumph as she said the last sentence – especially as the other four of us immediately screamed with excitement. "Oh wow!" I said, clapping my hands to the side of my face. "Thompsons' fruit and veg stall in Leicester market – I wonder if it's still there?"

"Brilliant detective work, Rosie," Lyndz said warmly.

"Grandpa reckons they were definitely still

there ten years ago," Rosie said, turning pink with pride at Lyndz's words. "He had an antiques stall there himself then. So what do you reckon – day trip to Leicester tomorrow? I've already asked my mum and she said I can go."

"Just try and stop me!" I said, jumping to my feet and bouncing up and down. "I've got a date with a fruit and veg stall – and wild horses couldn't keep me away!"

CHAPTER NINE

Wowee – so the hunt was back on! I was so excited by Rosie's news, I practically wet myself! It was such amazing news that the Thompsons had only moved down the road – it was going to be so much easier to find Vi now I knew she'd been living locally.

It was an absolutely gorgeous sunny day when we woke up on Saturday. Perfect detective weather – it made me want to get out of the house and start the hunt straight away. Mind you, Frankie's dad had different ideas, and served up this huge fried breakfast for us all. I have to say, the smell of bacon floating through the house was enough to make the keenest detective in the world sit down and tuck in!

Frankie's mum had already planned to go into Leicester as she wanted to change a pair of trousers she'd bought the week before. On Saturday mornings, Frankie's dad always looks after baby Izzy while Frankie's mum gets to do exactly what she feels like. Often she just stays in bed reading the newspapers and drinking coffee, but today she was up and about, and in the mood for some serious shopping. So we cadged a lift into town with her after breakfast.

The market was already heaving when we got there. There were so many stalls, we didn't know which end of the market to start. Meat stalls, fabric stalls, flower stalls, clothes stalls... The others all stopped in front of one stall selling bags of sweets and toffees and I practically had to drag them away with my bare hands. "Please can we look at the fruit and veg stalls first?" I had to remind them. "If we get anywhere with this, I promise I'll buy you all something from the sweet stall!"

We carried on making our way through the crowds – and then Rosie stopped dead and pointed straight ahead to a stall piled high with green and red apples, oranges, cabbages, broccoli and lettuces, with bananas swinging on hooks from the top of the stall. Excellent! We had to be close now!

Frankie went up to one of the men behind the stall. "We're looking for Thompsons' fruit and veg stall," she told him. "Do you know where it is?"

"What do you want to go there for?" he teased. "You won't get better prices than ours in the whole market. Four for a pound now, your apples!"

"We don't want to buy anything," I said hastily, "we're just looking for the Thompsons."

"Don't want to buy anything?" he asked, looking shocked. "Not even a nice bunch of bananas, ladies? Five for a pound – can't say fairer than that now!"

"No, not even bananas," I said. Was I going to have to spell it out to this man or what?

103

"Honestly – we're not going to buy anything from the Thompsons' stall either, we just want to know where they are."

"Honest?" he said, trying to wind us up. "You promise me you're not going to spend all your money buying their stock, not ours?"

"No!" we all shouted.

"Look, I'll buy a banana if you tell us," I said desperately, getting my purse out. "Just PLEASE tell us!"

He laughed then, and told me to put my purse away. "I was only pulling your leg," he grinned. "Here, help yourself to a few strawberries, girls. The Thompsons' stall is there – right in front of your nose!"

Typical! It WAS right in front of our noses, too – the next stall along, with THOMPSONS' written in huge letters over the top. Oops! How had Cuddington's finest detectives failed to miss THAT?

There were three people serving there. One sulky-looking teenage girl, and two men, about the same age as my dad – one of them with bright red hair! Frankie elbowed me as she clocked it at the same moment. "Check out Mr Ginger," she hissed. "He's GOT to be a relative!"

My heart was pounding so fast now, I barely tasted my strawberry as it slipped down my throat. I went straight up to the red-haired man. "Excuse me, I'm looking for Vi Thompson," I said, crossing my fingers behind her back. "I don't suppose you know her, do you?"

"Vi Thompson?" the red-haired man said, scratching his head and smiling in a friendly way. "No, I don't know any Vi Thompsons."

I just stared in disbelief. Not another dead end! "Oh," was all I could manage to say to that. I felt so disappointed. All my excitement just drained away at once.

The red-haired man smiled at the look on my face. "... But I do know a Vi Crossley, if that's any good," he continued. "She's my mum. Hasn't been called Vi Thompson for – ooh, about thirty-five years, ever since she married my dad!"

I could feel my eyes getting as big as saucers. "You mean..." I said, beaming at the others. "We've found her!" I yelled excitedly. "We've found Vi!"

The red-haired man stared at us as we all jumped up and down hugging each other and cheering. Come to think of it, quite a few people started staring at the five crazy girls bouncing around in front of a fruit and veg stall.

"Blimey, their prices must be good," one woman muttered curiously as she walked by.

"Hang on a minute," the red-haired man said. "You've lost me. How do you know my mum, then?"

"We don't," I said, "but my grandma does – they were best friends at school until they were about eleven, then your mum moved away and they lost touch. And I've been trying to find Vi to get them back together for our history project, and..."

Bit by bit, I managed to tell the whole story, with the others chipping in here and there with more details. By the time he'd got most of the facts, the red-haired man – whose name was Pete – was grinning away just as broadly as us.

"Well, I never!" he said. "Fancy that! My mum and your gran, eh?" Then he looked at his watch. "Well, girls, you're in luck. Mum always comes down at lunch time to cover our lunch breaks, so you can meet her for yourselves in an hour or two – how about that?"

"Awesome!" I breathed. "Thanks, Pete! We'll come back at twelve!"

As soon as we'd walked away from the stall, I threw my arms around Rosie, who looked a bit stunned. "This is all thanks to you and your brilliant grandad," I said happily. "The Sleepover Club have done it again!"

"What a result!" Frankie bubbled, looking just as excited as me. "I can't wait to see the look on Vi's face when she hears the story!"

Fliss looked at her watch and groaned. "We've got over an hour to kill first! What are we going to do?"

"Well, I seem to remember Kenz making a little promise," Lyndz said. "A little promise about some SWEETS after we found the fruit and veg stalls!"

"Absolutely!" I said, feeling wildly generous,

despite the fact that I only had about a pound on me. Who cared? It was my birthday soon – I'd have loads of money then. "Come on – sweets are on me!"

One hour and assorted jelly beans, cola bottles, white mice, chocolate buttons and toffees later, we went back to Pete's stall, feeling vaguely sick but majorly enthusiastic. I just hoped and hoped Pete hadn't given our surprise away to Vi – I so wanted to see her face when we told her the news!

But as it happened, we didn't even have to TELL her anything.

"That must be her!" I said, biting my lip with nerves as we went back to the stall. A sprightly-looking, white-haired lady was roaring with laughter about something or other as she served a customer. Pete caught sight of us and winked, motioning his head towards the lady, as if to say, "That's her!"

We walked towards Vi. But before I could even open my mouth to introduce myself, she stared at me and clapped a hand to her mouth. "Rose Sanders, as I live and breathe!"

she said, her blue eyes going very wide in surprise. "Pete, tell me I'm not seeing things!"

Pete chuckled. "Recognise her, do you, Mum?" he said. "Funny, that – she's come here to see you!"

Vi couldn't take her eyes off me. "The absolute spit," she murmured. "I'm right, aren't I? You MUST be related to Rose!"

"I'm her granddaughter," I said, unable to stop myself grinning like a loon. "And I'm VERY glad to meet you – we've been trying to track you down! Look!" I said, fishing out the newspaper clipping with a trembling hand. "I found this picture of the two of you!"

As Vi and Pete looked at the old clipping, Vi's eyes started to get a bit moist. Then she pulled out an enormous white hanky and blew her nose loudly. "Well, knock me down," she said, shaking her head. "Aren't you the spit of your granny, then? I thought I was seeing a ghost when you walked up to me!"

"Mum, how about you take these girls for a cup of tea and they'll tell you all about it?"

Pete said. "Go on – I can manage the stall for a bit."

So that was how we got to be sitting in Leicester market, having cups of tea and big slices of ginger cake with Vi Crossley, my grandma's long-lost friend. She couldn't stop hugging me at first and kept calling me 'Rose' by mistake, which was a bit weird! Then she made us tell her all about our long search to find her – and then she made me tell her about Grandma and Grandad and what they'd been doing all these years.

"She never married Bill Littler, did she?" Vi screeched, when I mentioned him. "Ooh, he was a wicked lad, always getting into trouble! Mind you – he was very handsome, I quite liked the look of him myself!"

When we'd finally told Vi all the gossip we could think of, she gave me another big hug and a smacking kiss on my head. "Laura, you've made my day," she said. "You've absolutely made my day – you're a lovely girl to think of getting us two old grannies back in touch again. I can't wait to see Rose and Bill now!"

I blushed bright red. "Well, shall we arrange a time and place?" I said quickly, to cover up how chuffed I was feeling. "How about Sunday dinner at ours tomorrow? Grandma and Grandad always come over for that – and then we can surprise them by having you walking in, too!"

"That sounds wonderful!" Vi said excitedly. "Oh, I hope I can wait until then!"

Once we'd swapped addresses and telephone numbers and she'd given me a few more enormous hugs and kisses, we said goodbye.

"Lovely to meet you all, girls," she said, as she put her money belt back on and went behind the fruit counter again. Then she gave me a broad wink. "And I'll see YOU tomorrow!"

CHAPTER TEN

I was just on cloud nine for the rest of the day. Even being dragged round all the clothes shops with Fliss couldn't wipe the smile off my face. We'd done it! We'd actually found Vi Thompson – and now she and Grandma were about to meet up again, after over fifty years of being apart. It was all just too awesome to take in!

The others kept teasing me for my permanent grin, but I didn't care. This time tomorrow, Grandma was going to get the surprise of her life – all down to me!

Mum was dead excited when I told her.

Even my yucky older sisters, Emma and Molly, wanted to hear the whole story and said, "Well done" and all that. Mum phoned Vi up that evening to make arrangements and give her directions to our house. Then all we had to do was wait...

Did I say I hate waiting for things? Oh yes, so I did. And this time was no exception. I was fidgeting around so much for the rest of the day that Dad took me out for a long run to try and tire me out. It helped a bit but, much as I love having my dad all to myself, going for a run together still wasn't enough to totally distract me. It wasn't just me, but my whole family that breathed a sigh of relief when it got to Sunday lunch time. At last Kenny Fidget-Knickers would sit still!

As we'd planned, Vi turned up at about twelve-thirty, before Grandma and Grandad were round. "I've hardly slept, I've been so looking forward to this!" she told us, with a twinkle in her eye.

Dad poured her a sherry to calm her nerves, and I went to keep guard by the window. "They're here!" I shouted excitedly when at long last, Grandad's old Renault parked outside. "Are you ready, Vi?"

"As I'll ever be!" she said, patting her hair into place.

The rest of us went to the front door to let Grandma and Grandad in, while Vi stayed at the dining table. Once Grandma and Grandad had hung their coats up, I took Grandma's arm. "I've got a little surprise for you," I said, smiling.

"Ooh, what's that, lovey?" she asked.

"It's not a what, it's a who," I said, leading her into the dining room. "Here she is!"

Vi stood up as we walked in. Her hands were trembling, and her face split into a huge grin. "Rose Sanders, as I live and breathe!" she said. "Remember me?"

Grandma gaped, and then blinked rapidly. "It's not... It can't be..." she said, a smile appearing on *her* face now. "It's never Vi Thompson!"

"The very same!" Vi said, rushing round the table.

Next thing, the two of them were hugging and laughing and both trying to talk at once.

"I can't believe it!"

"It's all thanks to Laura!"

"What a surprise!"

"I can't believe it myself!"

And then they were off... chat, chat, chat for the whole of Sunday dinner. It was amazing that either of them actually managed to eat any food, the amount of yakking that went on. When they'd calmed down a bit and dinner was all over, I got them to pose for a few photos and did some more interviewing for my history project. Boy, was I feeling proud of myself!

That Sunday was the start of the best week I'd had in absolutely ages. It was the last week at school before carnival and half-term, so everyone had that lovely winding-down feeling. We finished off various projects throughout the week, and then on Friday, we played lots of games and had class quizzes all day. If only school could be like that EVERY week, eh?

Then, on Saturday came the big day – the Cuddington carnival itself! Our class and Mr Phillips' class had to meet up in the playground in full costume, where a couple of mini buses were waiting to take us to our float. The only person who wasn't there was Lyndz – she was going to pick Alfie up and make her own way to the float. Frankie and Simon looked wicked for our team – and Fliss was a fantastic Sixties chick, too. There was a Twenties flapper, a Fifties teddy boy and girl, an Eighties New Romantic... everywhere you looked, there was someone in a wacky outfit.

The best bit was when we saw the float for the first time, waiting at the far end of the high street. It looked MEGA! Mrs Weaver and Mr Phillips had stuck all our banners on it, decade by decade, so that as you walked around it, you got a brilliant trip around the whole century. The models climbed up some folding steps – and then we were ready for the big off!

All the other floats were there too, so for those of us who weren't models or sweet throwers, we could have a wander round to check them out. It was awesome! There were a couple with steel bands on, one from the

116

bingo hall, a couple of farmers' floats with people dressed up as giant vegetables, one from Cuddington dairy with an enormous plastic cow in the middle, one with a load of ballerinas on... I couldn't wait for it all to begin now!

Lyndz trotted up on Alfie, smiling and waving at everyone. She'd put lots of plaits in Alfie's mane for the big occasion and looked pretty smart herself, in her jodhpurs, riding jacket and hat.

"Tally-ho!" I yelled when I saw her. "Chuck us a sweet, then, Lyndz!"

Boing! She threw me a jelly bean which bounced neatly off Rosie's head and on to the floor.

"Oops, sorry, Rosie!" Lyndz giggled. "I haven't got the hang of this yet!"

Rosie rubbed her head. "It might be safer if we just help ourselves from the box," she muttered to me as we went over.

"Actually, I hope this is going to be OK," Lyndz confided in us, once we were beside her. "Alfie absolutely loves barley sugar, and there's loads of it in this sweet box. He keeps getting dead excited, every time he gets a whiff."

"What, do you think he's going to charge someone down every time you throw them a barley sugar?" I asked, giggling at the thought. "That would be a bit of a nightmare, wouldn't it?"

"You're telling me," Lyndz said, quickly unwrapping a barley sugar for Alfie, as he tossed his head about and whinnied. "He's had five of them already and I only picked him up half an hour ago!"

Just then, someone blew a loud horn, and everyone went quiet. "I hereby declare the Cuddington Carnival... OPEN!" came a voice over the tannoy. "Let the parade begin!"

Everyone cheered and clapped as the first float set off down the street, and loads of different types of music started blasting out. After all the weeks of hard work, it was finally happening! The whole of the high street was suddenly full of bright colours, flashing lights, music, lovely food smells, you name it.

Our school float was about tenth from the

front, so we didn't have to wait too long before we could start moving. All the models started dancing as the engine started and we set off. Me and Rosie walked beside Lyndz, helping her throw sweets out to the cheering crowds. It was such fun hearing people's comments as we went by.

"One hundred years of Cuddington – ooh, look at that!"

"Look at that punk!"

"See that teddy girl? I used to dress up just like that!"

"Ooh dear, look, that girl's wig has just fallen off!"

Uh-oh! We turned round quickly to see who 'that girl' was – only to see Frankie with her Tina Turner wig halfway over her face! She'd been dancing so enthusiastically, it had come loose and slipped over her eyes. She told me later that she hadn't been able to see a thing, and had had to cling on to Simon to stop herself wobbling over on her high boots. She got a special cheer from the crowd when she'd pulled it over the right way, anyway, and it gave us a good laugh, too!

Once all the barley sugars had been thrown to people, Alfie calmed down and was back to being his usual, obedient self. Lyndz's aim didn't get any better and she managed to hit several people – including a policeman, right on his helmet!

"OOPS!" she said, going bright purple. "Sorry!"

There was so much to see and do! The market place was full of fairground rides and a big yellow bouncy castle, and the sides of the high street were lined with all sorts of different stalls, selling home-made cakes, arts and crafts, souvenirs and local produce. I couldn't wait to go off and have a good look at everything.

Then, in the crowd, I caught sight of Grandma and Grandad waving and cheering – and there was Vi next to them, with a red-headed girl about my age. As soon as Grandma saw me, she beckoned furiously for me to come over.

"Gotta go," I said to Rosie and Lyndz. "I'll catch up with you later!"

Grandma and Vi were all smiles when I went over. "You'll never guess who we've just been speaking to," Grandma said mysteriously.

"Oh, I don't know, Prince Charles?" I said. I hate guessing games! "Who?"

"Tell her, Vi," Grandma said, nudging her friend.

"A reporter from the *Leicester Mercury*," Vi said. "He thinks it's a brilliant story, the pair of us being reunited by you – and he wants to come round to interview all of us next week!"

"COO-ELL!" I shouted. "That's so fab! We're going to be famous!"

"And that's not all," Vi continued. "Tell her, Rose."

"The local radio station want to do a piece on the story too – and they want you and the Sleepover Club to go in and talk about your brilliant detective work!" Grandma said, squeezing my arm excitedly. "Who would have thought it, eh? All this from one old newspaper clipping that might never have been noticed!"

"Awesome!" I said. "Wait until I tell the

others!"

"Not so fast," Vi said. "There's someone here I'd like you to meet first – my granddaughter, Harriet!"

The red-headed girl stepped forward then and grinned, showing lots of gaps in her teeth. I'd never seen anyone with so many freckles in my life!

"I love your Leicester City top," she said at once. "C'mon, you Foxes!"

"You're a footy fan, too?" I said, liking her immediately. "Excellent!"

"That's not the only thing you two have got in common," Grandma said mysteriously. "You're the same age, too! Harriet, when's your birthday?"

Harriet gave her gran a funny look. "The ninth of June, of course," she said, frowning. "What is all this?"

"That's my birthday, too!" I said, staring at her in shock. "We were born on exactly the same day!"

"Same day – and same hospital, no less!" Grandma said. "Can you believe it? Me and Vi probably passed each other in the hospital corridor, all those years ago! You might even have been in the next bed! Isn't that a coincidence?"

"That is so cool!" I said, shaking my head and grinning.

"That is AWESOME!" Harriet said, her eyes goggling. "We're practically twins!"

The four of us – young, old, young, old – stood in a circle, smiling and looking amazed. And I suddenly got a real sense of what Mrs Weaver had been trying to teach us about. History! And without wanting to sound like a complete swot, I decided that history could be pretty funky at times.

"Come on, then, you lot!" I smiled, linking arms with Harriet and Grandma. "What are we waiting for? Let's party!"

And that, I'm afraid, really is the end of the story. Just to say that the carnival was an absolute blinder and I'm hoping now that the Powers That Be decide to put one on every year, after this one was such a roaring success. Still, there are lots of other things to look forward to now – going on local radio, and getting my ugly mug in the newspaper, for example. How ace is that?

Also, me and Harriet have promised to keep in touch, just like Grandma and Vi. The four of us are going to try and meet up either in Cuddington or Leicester. And Harriet's dead keen for us to go to some football matches with our dads too, so that will be wicked. As Grandma said, who would have thought that an old newspaper clipping could mean such exciting things happening to all of us?

Anyway, I'd better go – I'm in trouble again, for bashing one of the wing mirrors on Dad's car with a cricket bat. I'm sad to say, I've got LOADS of chores to do as a punishment. Ooh – I think I just heard Mum shouting for me to come and help her hang the washing out, so I must dash. SIGH! No rest for the wicked, as Frankie would say!

This is Kenny McKenzie saying a big fat cheerio with a cherry on top. See you soon!

The Sleepover Club on the Beach

A long weekend of camping by the seaside offers a few surprises for the Sleepover Club. Their first surprise is that there are no funfairs or arcades near the campsite – boring! But then they find a mysterious message in a bottle, washed up by the tide...

Roll up your combats and paddle on over!

Order Form

To order direct from the publishers, just make a list of the titles you want and fill in the form below:

Name ....

Address ....

....

....

Send to: Dept 6, HarperCollins Publishers Ltd, Westerhill Road, Bishopbriggs, Glasgow G64 2QT.

Please enclose a cheque or postal order to the value of the cover price, plus:

UK & BFPO: Add £1.00 for the first book, and 25p per copy for each additional book ordered.

Overseas and Eire: Add £2.95 service charge. Books will be sent by surface mail but quotes for airmail despatch will be given on request.

A 24-hour telephone ordering service is available to holders of Visa, MasterCard, Amex or Switch cards on 0141- 772 2281.

Collins
An *Imprint of* HarperCollins*Publishers*